The Boy Who Cried Wolf

An imprint of Om Books International

There once lived a naughty shepherd boy named Ralph. He was still a wee lad and wanted to jump around, play and do no real work. But alas! He was made to take the boring sheep out to graze in the green meadows every single day!

"Oh, I'm bored, I'm bored, I'm bored," he sang in a sad little voice one afternoon. He sat and wondered, then stood up and wondered and finally, lay down and wondered what he could do. And then an idea struck him.

"WOLF! IT'S A WOLF!" he cried at the top of his lungs.

"Somebody save my sheep! Baaaaah! The big bad wolf is going to get me...HEEELLLLP!"

The village baker, the mayor, the butcher and the wagoner, all ran out with rakes and muskets, ready to beat up the bad mean wolf.

But what was this? What did they all see once they reached Ralph? The naughty lad was rolling with laughter in the grass!

"Oh that was such great fun!" he said, "I fooled you all – there is no wolf."

The men all muttered – mutter, mutter, mutter. And then they grumbled – grumble, grumble, grumble. The villager in the funny red breeches grumbled the most.

"Hmph!" they said in unison, and tucking away their weapons they all went away.

There was no stopping Ralph, however. Every time he was bored, every time the sun, the clouds, the birds and the bees couldn't entertain him, he would go back to his silly trick.

"WOLF! HELP! WOLF!" he would scream again, and the village folk would come whooshing like the wind.

Where was the wolf? There was no wolf! So, all the grumbling and muttering would happen again, but what was the use of it all? The kid had to be told to behave himself.

"Look here, my boy," said the baker to Ralph, "It's very bad to play pranks like this. Wolves are dangerous animals and you must not jest about one. Now we won't come to your rescue even if there is a real wolf after your back!"

But Ralph paid no attention. Surely
no big bad wolf would come after him!

Alas! How wrong little Ralph was to think no wolf would come.

One bright, sunny day, Ralph heard a "GRRROWL" and a "SLURRRP" and a howl go "OOOoooOOOOoooo"!

The big bad wolf was here! My oh my, who would save the sheep now?

As the wolf came running towards Ralph and his sheep, Ralph ran down the meadow slopes at top speed!

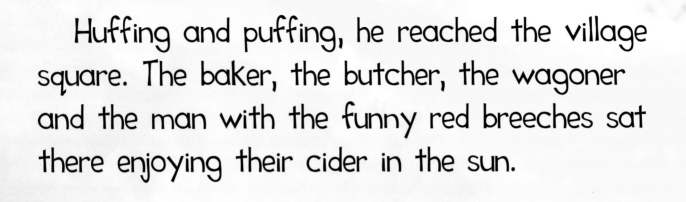

Huffing and puffing, he reached the village square. The baker, the butcher, the wagoner and the man with the funny red breeches sat there enjoying their cider in the sun.

"Wolf...huff...huff...help!" cried Ralph, but not a soul paid attention.

Poor Ralph! He couldn't do a thing. Nobody believed him now and they continued to make merry, while the wolf in the meadow enjoyed a delicious feast!